Christmas Kitten

Story and Pictures
by
Wanda Snow Porter

To furry friends
who bring so much joy

Big eyes peered through the living room window.

"It's the kitten I asked Santa for," Lilly squealed. She opened the door, and the kitten scampered inside.

"What?" Mom said. "Christmas is a day away."

Lilly picked up the kitten and hugged her. "Her name will be Catherine the Great," she said.

"Don't get too excited," Mom said. "She may belong to a neighbor."

Lilly crossed her fingers when Mom asked everyone in the neighborhood about Catherine.

No one had lost a kitten.

Mom and Lilly went to the pet store and bought kitty toys, bowls, and a litter box.

Mom told Lilly, "Santa expects you to feed Catherine and clean her litter box every day."

Lilly nodded and said, "I promise."

Lilly put Catherine's litter box in the laundry room.

She filled one kitty bowl with water and another with kitten chow.

The hungry and thirsty kitten lapped the water and ate her meal.

Then Catherine followed Lilly into her bedroom to play.

The next morning, Lilly hurried to a friend's house to take her a gift. She forgot to feed Catherine.

Lilly returned home late that afternoon. The kitten's water and food bowls were empty.

"Kitty, kitty, kitty," she called.

Catherine did not come.

Lilly looked under tables and beds and inside closets.

An open window alerted her to look outside.

Lilly looked and looked.

She found no kitten.

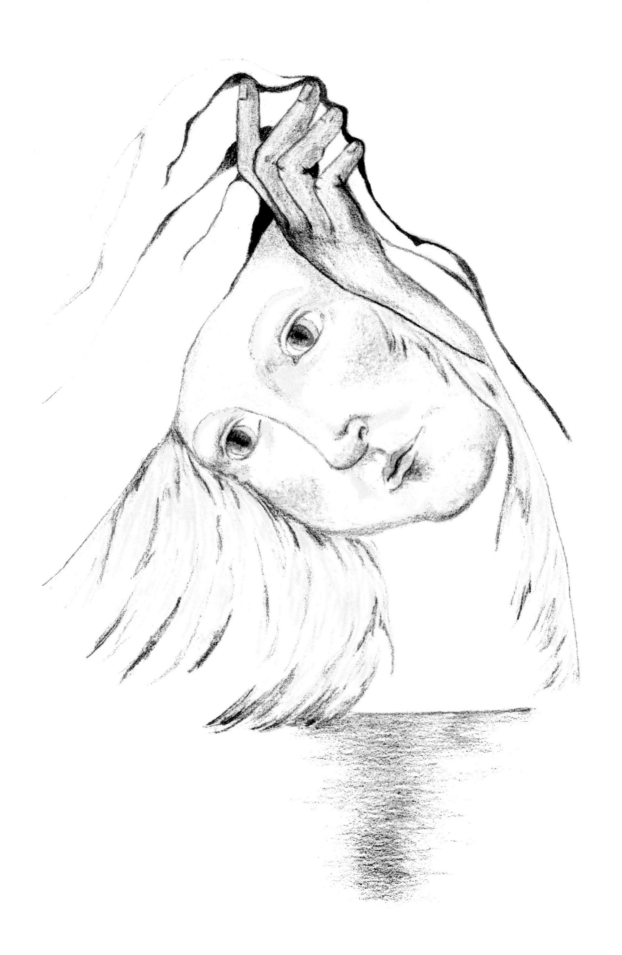

Lilly walked to the park. There, six cats surrounded a plump man with a white beard.

One was Catherine.

While the cats yowled, he wrote in a notepad.

Was he Santa?

Were the cats homeless? Were they asking him to give them a child for Christmas?

Did Catherine tell Santa about her empty food bowl? Would Lilly now be on his naughty list?

She waved at Santa and called, "Catherine."

The kitten followed Lilly home and hurried to her empty bowls.

She stared up at Lilly and meowed.

Lilly peered into Catherine's eyes.

"I'm sorry," she cried. "Forgive me, Catherine. I will never forget you again."

Lilly filled the kitten's food and water bowls. She cleaned the litter box and shut all the windows.

That night was Christmas Eve. Lilly and Catherine snuggled in bed to await Santa's visit.

The kitten purred, and Lilly whispered, "Naughty list or not, Santa already brought me the greatest gift ever. I love you, Catherine."

Made in the USA
Las Vegas, NV
11 December 2020